Whore To Holiness

Lillie R. Lee

ENTEGRITY CHOICE PUBLISHING

Entegrity Choice Publishing
PO Box 453
Powder Springs, GA 30127
info@entegritypublishing.com

Book Cover Designed by: Kylie Dalton

ISBN: 978-0-9974859-7-4

Library of Congress Control Number: 2017942146

Printed in the United States of America

Acknowledgements

I give all thanks to God for bringing me out from my pain, suffering, and struggle. I am grateful that you kept me in spite of my sins. When people turned their backs on me, you were always there.

I thank you Lord for keeping the enemies' hand off of me. When I disobeyed, you still loved me and never left me. Many times I wanted to give up and commit suicide, but your Spirit was with me and stopped me. I am so blessed to have you as my father.

Contents

Introduction

This book is about the life of a little girl named Natasha, who lived in a life where love never existed. One thing she knew for certain was God's unwavering love for her. Despite making some bad decisions, she knew that God's hand was always upon her life, and she loved Him with all of her heart.

Church was her "go-to" place for peace. Slowly, Satan used her desire to be free from her troubled home life to his advantage. She began partying, drinking, and sleeping with men just to find love. Her story will take you on a roller coaster ride. At times, it will have you laughing and crying at the same time. These pages contain her journey from whore to holiness. It is her desire that this book inspire you to believe that no matter what life throws at you, you can always get back up.

1

First Sunday

Waking up to the smell of bacon, eggs, grits, and biscuits was habitual at our house on Sundays.

The smell of breakfast signaled that it was "church day." Going to church was a family ritual; we wouldn't miss it. The day started with Sunday school and then worship service. I used to say to myself, "With all of the church and praying up in this house, I know I'm going to heaven."

As I was getting out of bed, I noticed that Mom had laid out that ugly flower dress that I hated for church. I hated the dress because it looked like an old lady's dress. Sadly, I had to wear it.

While I was agonizing over the dress, Mom yelled, "Breakfast is ready, get down here." I ran to see if my sister and brother were up. I found my sister up and getting ready. When I went past my brother's room, he was sleeping. I shook him and said, "Get up before Mom comes up here with that belt."

My brother was spoiled rotten; Mom let him do whatever he wanted, probably because he was the only boy. I really didn't like how he was the favorite child, but I was powerless to change it. On the other hand, my sister had a bad attitude towards me. Often, it appeared that she hated me. Nonetheless, I loved her.

I finished getting dressed and went downstairs for breakfast. When Mom saw me, she asked, "Where is your sister and brother?" I said, "Rose is in the bathroom finishing up her hair, and Lil' John is still in the bed. I tried to get him up, but he didn't move." We were not allowed to start eating until everybody was at the table. That was Mom's rule, and she didn't bend it.

Five minutes later, my siblings came running down the stairs. My Mom asked, "What took you two so long? Why do Natasha beat you two downstairs every Sunday? Let this be the last Sunday that this happens."

Dad came to the table, looked at me, and said, "Are you ready, Natasha?" He asked me that because I was giving my life to Jesus and getting baptized. I was excited and nervous at the same time. I shook my head and replied, "Yes sir, but a little nervous." My mom said, "You will be OK." That day, I knew in my heart that I loved Jesus Christ and I was going to serve Him until I died. I knew that God was going to use me one day.

Dad blessed the food; "Lord, thank you for this breakfast that my beautiful wife has fixed for us; in Jesus' name I pray." Mealtime was the most important family time of the day for us. We usually talked and prayed, but something was not right in the house.

Everyone was almost finished with breakfast when Mom blurted out, "It is time to go. We don't want to be late for church and Natasha's baptism." I just smiled. I knew my sister was getting jealous, but I didn't care because that day was all about me.

The kids ran to get in our long, brown station wagon; it had three rows of seating. I loved sitting in the last back row of the car. People used to call us the Brady Bunch. Perhaps it was our station wagon that prompted the nickname, but I didn't care.

When we arrived at church, the parking lot was full. I remember thinking, "These people are here to see me." You could hear the choir from the parking lot. The First Baptist Church had the best choir in town.

When we walked in the church, Pastor Green was starting to preach, and the old heads were shouting away. It was a wonderful service. Pastor Green's sermon was "How to love your enemies." As I was enjoying the service, an old lady tapped me on the shoulder and asked me to come with her. We went to the back of the church, and she put a white robe on me and covered my head with a white headscarf. I was a little nervous, but I knew I was doing this because Jesus Christ died on the cross for me so that I could have everlasting life.

I walked up a hallway and a door opened. I could see Pastor Green standing with his hand out guiding me into the baptismal pool. He began to pray, and then he dipped my head into the cold water. Immediately, I knew that I was a child of God. The whole church was shouting, praying, and clapping for me. I could see my mom crying.

I loved church; it was my outlet. I sang in the youth choir and had to be on the front row. I was the loudest singer. My favorite song was

"God, Open Up the Windows of Heaven." At a young age, I knew that God was going to use me in a special way. I didn't know what He was going to do, but I knew I was going to be used.

2

Where Is The Love?

I was a loner; therefore my imagination soared. I had this crazy imagination that I was a little rich kid. In my imaginary rich world, I lived the following fantasy: I lived in a big beautiful house with a perfect family where there was no fighting, screaming, or cursing. Mom took me shopping and bought me the latest fashion. I had the perfect dad. When I saw my dad, he delighted in me running and jumping into his arms, and he told me that I was pretty and special. We had a live-in chef that cooked fabulous meals, and I had a personal maid. Having a personal maid was awesome. All I had to do was ring my silver bell, and the maid would check on me. We took family vacations at least twice a month. Dad owned a black private jet. Mom took the kids shopping and spent $3,000 on us. Mom often said that she loved us so much and that's why she did it. I loved pretty dresses and shoes. I had one hundred pairs of shoes and dresses, but I still wanted more. One time I imagined my family stayed a week in Hawaii.

What a life! I often escaped into my private fantasy world, which was a temporary relief from the drama around me. Living in a fantasy world was depressing when I woke up to my reality. I remember having one of my imaginary dreams when I was interrupted by loud yelling. Mom could yell very loud. Yelling, screaming, and cursing were normal noises in my home. Often, I played outside, building grass houses just to get away from the noise. We lived in the projects, but it wasn't so bad. People in the community got along, but occasionally kids got into fights. I remember one family in particular whose kids were horrible. Often, they would try to bully me and my siblings, but it wouldn't go down. My brother was a fighter. He didn't take mess from no one.

One time this boy and his sister tried to jump on my brother. My brother beat them both at the same time. My big brother was tough, and I looked up to him. I knew God was looking down over me, but I just couldn't find Him. I used to wonder, "Why me, Lord?", but I got no answer. I used to be jealous of other little girls because they had pretty clothes and stayed in a nice home. I just hated myself. I did not understand why God put me in this hellish family. God never answered me.

My life sucked. I wore ugly clothes, lived in rundown project housing, and my parents fought constantly. At times, I made the best of it. Some days me and my friends got together and played kickball. I also loved playing double-dutch. We didn't have a real jump rope so we used a hose pipe. I could jump for hours.

Mom was a disciplinarian; sometimes I thought we were in jail. All I could say was, "Why me, Lord?" My dad worked for the city, driving a garbage truck. When he came through our neighborhood to collect garbage, we ran outside to make sure he saw us so that he would blow the horn. I had a big smile on my face, but deep down inside I was crying. I wanted my dad to love me. I felt no love from him. I longed to run and jump in my daddy's lap. I liked calling my grandparents just to see how they were doing, but especially to talk to my grandfather. He nicknamed me "Talker" because I could talk for hours. I thought it was funny. One day my grandfather said, "Talker, you should be a lawyer." "Why, Grandfather?," I asked. He said, "You ask a million questions and can talk the horns off someone." I laughed and laughed when he teased me.

One day I answered the phone, and all I could hear was screaming and crying. I thought it was someone playing on the phone, but it was my aunt. She called to tell us that Granddaddy just died. I couldn't believe what I was hearing, so I dropped the phone and ran to my grandparents' house. When I got there, cars were everywhere. I wanted to know what happened. My aunt said, "He died sitting on the back porch singing, 'Swing Low, Sweet Chariot' and then he went to heaven." I overheard my grandmother tell my uncle that Grandfather ate breakfast and then went outside to cut wood to make sure there was wood in the house and a pile outside of the house. Afterwards, he went out back, sat down, and started singing. When she went to check on him, she could not wake him.

That day I lost more than a grandfather; I lost my best friend. He was the only person that understood me. On the day of the funeral, you would think that the President of the United States had died because there were so many people. A lot of people loved my grandfather, and they came to show their love. I have nothing but good memories about my grandfather. I just couldn't understand why God took him away from me since I felt lonely and lost in this so-called world. My grandfather had so much wisdom and knowledge. I heard that he didn't have any education and in spite of that, he was smart. He was seven feet tall and dark as night with a smile that could light up a room. People had so many nice words to say about him. I wanted to go where God had taken my grandfather. I hid my grief from my family. I didn't want anyone to see me crying and ask what was wrong.

Following my grandfather's death, one day my dad needed to go back to his hometown to bring an old car to get it fixed. My dad's friend, "Junebug," chained the old car to dad's car to tow it. My sister, brother, and I asked Dad if we could go because we could pick berries, peaches, and run around and play. Dad said yes, and we were so excited. As we began the trip, it seemed as though we were traveling on the hottest day of the year. We did not have air in the car, so we rolled down the windows.

My dad's step-mom rode with us just to get out of the house. My step-grandma came often and stayed months at a time. We enjoyed her stay. My step-grandma was a little bossy, but I just overlooked what she said sometimes. I was sneaky at times, and that was my way of getting back at her. At times, I put salt in her water when she tried to boss me.

The road trip was nice. Of course, I did all the talking. As we were riding, I felt a tap behind us from the car we were towing. I asked my dad if he felt the tap, and he said that everything was all right. We were about ten miles down the road when we crossed a high bridge. Suddenly, I felt a bang and realized that the car behind us had hit us. Our car crashed hard into the wall of the bridge. The kids began screaming, " Dad, Dad!" I was crying and my lip was bleeding badly. I looked up and saw my grandmother's head open. Junebug was bleeding, but he made the rounds to ask if everybody was all right. I saw a police car approaching. The officer yelled, "Help is on the way." The ambulance arrived about forty-five minutes later.

3

God Came And Left

My uncle went to my mom's job to tell her about the accident. We made it to the Emergency Room; my father, brother, and sister were hurt badly. Junebug had minor injuries. My grandmother didn't make it. I told the doctor who everyone was because I only had a busted lip. My mom ran into the Emergency Room screaming, "Is everybody OK? Where's my family? What happened?" I ran to hug Mom, and the doctor tried to calm her down.

That day was a total disaster. God came on the scene and left me speechless. After the car wreck, life in my family was very different; I felt different. I wondered as a child if God was trying to tell me something. I just couldn't map it out. We went to Applewood, Alabama, to bury Grandma. We really didn't cry; no one did but Dad. I guess he took it hard because his real mother had left him to go upstate after a band member, and she had become his mother.

One thing I can say about Mom and Dad is that they were some hard working people. They didn't have a lazy bone in their bodies. Sometimes Mom would let us stay at Auntie Loulou's house in the projects. Her home was worse than ours, but we loved going to see her. Auntie Loulou was a great cook. As a matter of fact, she could cook better than Mom. Her potato salad was to die for. My auntie's house was strange. She had rats and roaches so bad that they didn't go and hide when people came over. You would think they were family members.

One day auntie Loulou had a cookout with ribs, chicken, hot dogs, baked beans, my favorite potato salad, and grape Kool-Aid. I wanted seconds, so I looked in the stove to get some food and saw a rat run across the meat. Do you know what I did? I got a piece of meat because the food was so good I didn't care about a big brown rat. Auntie Loulou's house always had a lot of food. I think she received food stamps because at times she would give us brown and green money that had a big $1.00 sign on it.

My auntie had this old blue truck, and we rode on the back of it when she went to the grocery store. I loved going to Piggly Wiggly. She let us eat chips and cookies in the store. I had the best time at my auntie's house. She was also a very wise woman. She told me, "Never let a man beat you." I wished she would tell my mom that because I was so sick and tired of the fighting at my house. I wished my mother was as strong as her sister. If Mom was stronger, she could stop my dad from beating her. My auntie was a very tall woman with brown skin and very strong. One time a man tried to slap her, and she threw him into the wall.

Auntie had three children, and they were my favorite cousins. They were much older than me. I used to wish to be their age because they could hang out late. The only thing I didn't like about visiting my auntie's house was seeing a crazy, light-skinned man named Joe that lived with her. He paid my auntie to stay in her house. He looked sneaky and made me nervous when he looked at us. One day my cousin and I were watching TV when I looked over at Joe and saw his zipper open. His manhood was sticking out of his pants. I had never seen a real man's private parts, only the ones in the porn movies I sneaked and watched that were under my dad's bed.

While we were watching TV, Joe called my cousin and me over to sit on his lap. I was scared out of my mind. He asked us if we wanted to play with his snake in his pants. He put my hand on top of his privates. He said, "Rub it, do you like it?" My cousin had looked like a deer in the headlights, but I did what he asked because he was a mental patient. I felt nasty, but I didn't know who to tell. Who would believe me? I asked myself, "God, do you see this? Help me." Joe wanted me to play with his private parts when no one was around. I liked it, but at times it made me feel sick. One day I asked my auntie, "Where is Joe?" She said, "He died last night." I could have jumped over the hills when I heard that he was dead. I was sick of playing with his private parts. I asked her if she was OK, but in my heart I was happy that nasty dog was gone.

One day my auntie took sick, and no one knew what was going on. It was in the spring and the weather was nice outside. She stayed in bed a lot, and her skin began to get darker. Soon she couldn't get out of bed. Mom stayed overnight to take care of her. Once, I overheard her son tell his friend that Auntie had sugar diabetes. I really didn't know what that was. In my mind, I thought it meant that Auntie ate a lot of sugar.

It was one cold winter morning when Auntie had to be rushed to the Emergency Room. My heart hit the floor. Mom didn't let me go with them. I was so mad at my mom, but I knew if I said something smart, there would have been some yelling going on. That day, I stayed by the phone, waiting on someone to call and let me know how Auntie was doing. Around 10:30 p.m., the phone rang, and when I answered, I immediately asked, "What's going on? How is she doing?" I did not get a response. About thirty seconds later, I heard a voice say, "She gone." I dropped the phone and ran in the closet and cried. I asked God, "Why? Why did you do this? My auntie was all I had to hold me down. She gave me my strength, and now she is gone." It was then that I knew that God never loved me. After the death of my aunt, I felt empty and lost. I had no one to tell how I was feeling. She was my safe haven. Repeatedly I asked, "Why, God?"

Letter to Auntie Loulou,

Thank you for your love. Thank you for opening up your door and making me feel safe. Thank you for feeding me and teaching me. So, wherever you may be, I know you are flying like an eagle.

Love, Natasha

4

Suffering Inside

I vividly remember that it was cold outside when the school bell rang for Christmas break As everyone was leaving school, I heard the kids talking about what they were going to get for Christmas. I wished I could have gone home with my best friend, Kim, for Christmas.

Kim and I were in the sixth grade. She lived in a nice house with both of her parents. She had a small dog, and sometimes my mom would let me spend the night with Kim. Her bedroom was big, and her mother painted her room purple and lavender. She had all the clothes and shoes that a little girl could wear. She was the best dressed in school. I was so jealous of her, but she didn't know it because I played it off. Kim could run and hug her dad, and he kissed her back. I would give a trillion dollars to run and hug my dad. My dad never showed any affection towards me.

One day when I was visiting Kim, I stole some of her panties when she wasn't looking. She had at least 50 pairs of panties; she wouldn't miss them. Kim's family took lots of summer vacations. I never asked Kim to spend the night at my house because I was ashamed of where I lived. My bedroom was not as pretty as Kim's, but I did keep it clean. Constantly, I asked myself, "Why did God put me with this dysfunctional family?" I did not get an answer. Kim lived five miles from my house. Often I walked with her about halfway to her house after school. She had a boyfriend named Willie, and he was cute. I hated it when Willie came around; I wanted it to be Kim and me only.

I hated boys; I thought they were ugly. They were even uglier to me after I played with Joe's private parts. Not only did I think boys were ugly, I was ugly, too. One day I was walking home in the cold from Kim's house and looked down at my feet. I had on the ugliest shoes a girl could wear. They were black and shiny. You'd think I was getting ready for a Michael Jackson video.

Mom bought our clothing from garage sales. I hated going to garage sales on Saturdays. I wanted to ask Mom, "Why do we have to wear other people's clothes and shoes? Why can't we go to the department stores like other kids' parents?" I knew better than to ask those questions because I would get yelled at. A kid in my school talked bad about my clothes and shoes and on top of that I had a jheri curl. Sometimes I put too much soft sheen spray on it, and it ran down my neck. The soft sheen spray made my hair look greasy constantly. The kids at school also teased me because of the clothes that I wore. I will never forget when a boy named Keith came behind me and started touching my pants leg saying, "Ring, Ring." I had on bell-bottom pants. I ran in the bathroom and cried. That day, I wanted to kill myself, but I didn't know how.

Five days before Christmas, I was in bed and was awakened by screaming and crying. I wondered, "Am I dreaming?" I ran downstairs and found my dad beating my mom's head into the wall. Blood was running down her face, and she was screaming, "Stop, stop!" I screamed, "Daddy, stop, Daddy, stop." My brother tried to stop my dad, and I ran to call 911. When the 911 operator answered, she asked, "What is your emergency?" I screamed, "My dad is killing my mommy, please come." She asked for my address. I said, "80L Project Hill- please hurry." She asked me for my name, and I replied, "Natasha." The 911 operator kept asking me stupid questions, and by the time the police arrived, my brother had broken up the fight.

I wanted the police to take my dad to jail for what he did to my mom. The officer asked, "What's going on?" I heard my dad say, "Nothing, Mr. Officer, just a little misunderstanding." My mom didn't say a word. She stood staring as if she had seen a ghost. I wanted to know why Mom didn't say something to the police or why didn't she fight back like my auntie.

The police spoke to my parents and afterwards said, "If we have to come back out here, someone is going to jail." We went back into the house. Mom sat on her bed silently, and I asked her if she was all right. She looked at me and smiled. I hated my dad. A short time later, Mom began to fix dinner. The whole night you could hear a rat move. I was so scared. Living at home, all I could do was pray. I prayed, "Father God, where are you? Do you hear my cries, God?" Amen.

5

No Santa Claus

I hated when my dad's friends stopped by the house. The only thing they did was sit on the porch and get drunk. Beer and gin were their favorite drinks. I remember on one occasion Dad asked me to pour him a drink. I went in the kitchen and pulled out a bottle of gin Dad had in the closet and poured him a drink. I was very curious so I took a sip. Not too bad I thought. Before I knew it, I had taken ten sips. The alcohol made me feel as if I was going around in circles, and my head was spinning. I wondered what was going on with me, but I played it off. When I gave Dad the glass of gin, he didn't ask what took me so long because he was too busy talking. I didn't like my dad's friend nicknamed Pig. We never knew his real name, but he made me sick. When Pig got drunk, he started spitting when he talked. I just wished he would go home.

Christmas was around the corner, and I was looking forward to some nice gifts that this man called Santa Claus was bringing. I was told that he was a fat, white man with a long, grey beard, red suit, and had reindeers. He was supposed to bring my gifts down the chimney. What a lie! We didn't have a chimney living in the projects, so how was he going to get to my hood? I went along with the lie; it was all in fun. Mom asked us what we all wanted for Christmas. My brother Lil' John said, "I want a Michael Jackson coat and some new Nikes." My sister, Kate, said, "Give me $100 and I'm good." When Mom got to me, I said, "I want purple skates, five new dresses, a black pair of Nikes, and six new pairs of blue jeans." I also told Mom that I had seen a really nice radio that I wanted and make sure to tell Santa that I want the Rodeo Red radio. My friend Kim had the same radio in her room, but hers was green. I think a lot of girls had this type of radio. It wasn't too big or too small; it was a nice size that played all kinds of music. The cool thing about the radio was a light on the side that lit up at night. Mom had a crazy look on her face after we told her what we wanted for Christmas. I didn't know what her facial expression meant. Anyway, I went upstairs to go to bed. Before going to bed, I prayed, "God, please let me get everything that I asked for Christmas. I am so sick of wearing used clothes and kids talking about me. Please do it, God. Amen."

The next morning, I went downstairs to see if Santa left me what I asked for. Mom was cooking breakfast as usual. She pointed to the

Christmas tree and told me to go see what Santa left me. I ran over and began opening a big box. I was so happy. As I was opening the box, I prayed, "My radio, please let it be in this box." When I got the box opened, I pulled out an ugly little radio. My eyes swelled with tears. Under the radio was only two pairs of jeans, and they were ugly too. I asked God, "Did you hear me last night or did you fall asleep while I was talking to you?" I wanted to cry and fall out, but I played it off. I told Mom that something was in my eye, and I ran to the bathroom and cried my eyes out. I heard my sister and brother come downstairs to open their gifts. I heard Mom tell them, "When things get a little better with my finances, I will take you shopping and get you what you didn't get for Christmas." Unfortunately, things never got better. I wanted to run away and never look back.

I was sick and tired of not having money, so I started stealing from my dad. While Dad was asleep in bed, I eased into his room and pulled $40 out of his wallet. Once, after stealing money, I went to the mall. I ate at the Food Court and bought some lip gloss. I was one happy girl but deep down inside, I felt bad. Stealing from my dad became a bad habit. Dad always accused Mom of taking his money, but I took it: $20 here, $60 there, every week.

One time I was looking for Dad's wallet, and I ran across tapes that had naked people on them in a sexual way. I put the tape in my shirt. My sister and brother were doing their own thing, Mom was at work, and Dad had left the house. I put the tape in the VCR and turned it on. My mouth dropped. There were two people having sex. I was thinking to myself, "How could a man's penis feel good inside of me?" I played with one and got sick, but watching porn made me want one. While watching the video, a feeling came over me that made me feel good.

Slowly, I became hooked on watching porn. I really didn't pray like I should have, but deep down inside; I had a strange feeling, but I couldn't put my finger on it. He didn't answer my prayers, so I didn't need God. This became my new attitude, so I decided to figure out this thing called life on my own.

6
Felt Love

I was determined that I was not going to high school wearing other people's ugly clothes. I needed money to buy clothes, so I thought about stealing more money from Dad each week but later changed my mind.

After thinking about several ideas on how to make money, I decided to ask the old ladies in the project if I could clean or do odd work around their homes. I liked to watch the old ladies in church. They were always friendly towards me, and that made me feel good inside. One little old lady named Mrs. Lucy told me that she prays for me because God is going to use me in a special way. I always smiled when she said those words; however, in my mind, I knew that God didn't love me. God never answered my prayers, so He could leave me alone. I made $40 a week by knocking on old ladies' doors, and in addition to the $40, I stole from my dad. Strangely, I kept feeling funny, like something was pulling at me, but I didn't pay it any attention because I wanted what I wanted.

Having money put me in the game. When Mom gave me permission to go with Kim and her mom to the mall school shopping, I was on cloud nine. I had earned and stolen money and had about $200 to spend. Two hundred dollars made me feel like a million dollars. That day, I bought three pairs of jeans and four shirts. Kim's mom bought me two pairs of shoes. I was going to look good in high school.

On the first day of school, I was happy. I had new clothes and new shoes. I was "feeling myself" as I walked into school. I enjoyed showing off my new clothes. With the excitement, I was still nervous because a lot of kids lived in my project. I saw Kim and she looked beautiful. Her outfit was amazing. Her hair was laced with gorgeous curls. I told Kim that she looked nice. She returned the compliment, but I didn't believe her. I always thought I was ugly and fat.

Kim's boyfriend, Joe, went to the same high school. He really made me sick, but only because he took Kim's attention away from me. In high school, I started thinking that I would like to have a boyfriend. There were a lot of cute boys at school. As I was walking to class one day, a tall, light- skinned boy caught my attention. He was walking my way, and I pretended that I didn't see him. As he walked past me, he said, "Hey, what's your name?" I turned around and looked him right in his eyes and asked, "Are you talking to me?" He said, "Yes, what is your name?" I said, "Natasha Lee and yours?" "Mark Brown, it's nice to meet you," he responded. He started talking, and I was melting as he spoke. He told me that he saw me across the hall, and my smile caught his eye. He told me that I have a very pretty smile. I said, "Thank you." I asked him what grade he was in, and he replied, "12th grade." His name was Mark. He was so tall; I had to look up at him. He asked me for my number and I gave it to him.

When the bell rang, it was time to get to my next class. Mark asked if he could walk me to class, but I told him no, because I could not let Mark know that I was in Special Ed for math. My learning was slow in math, and I needed that one-on-one attention. Sitting in math class, I couldn't stop thinking about that cutie I met in the hallway. Suddenly, I started thinking crazy thoughts: I wondered why he liked me because I was ugly. Out of all the pretty girls at this school, why did he ask for my number? Nevertheless, it felt good to be liked. Finally, school was over, and it was time to go home. Kim gave me a ride home because I didn't feel like walking home on the first day of school. I saw Mark get on the school bus. Someone told me that Mark played on the varsity basketball team; therefore, I was going to try-out for the girls' basketball team. I just needed to know the date for tryouts.

About forty-five minutes after I got home, the phone rang, and I answered it. A voice said, "Hey, what's up?" I didn't recognize the voice so I asked, "Who is this?" "Natasha, this is Mark," he said. "Oh, hey, what's up with you?" I asked. Mark said, "Before I started my homework, I wanted to call you." I had a big Kool-Aid smile on my face. We talked for two hours about church and what foods we liked. He asked me where I lived, which led us to discover that we lived about twenty minutes apart. We also learned that we both go to the same church, although I have never seen him there. I told him that I heard that he plays ball. He said, "Yeah, I do a little something."

Mark asked me if I had a boyfriend. I said, "No." He blurted out, "Why not?" I didn't know how to answer him. He said, "As pretty as you are, boys should be all over you." Well, they aren't," I replied. I wanted to say that I never had a boyfriend nor have I ever kissed a boy before.

I was thinking to myself, "I have played with a man's penis when I was younger." Mark told me that he liked me and wanted to see where it goes.

Our conversation was interrupted because Mom came home. That evening, I couldn't stop thinking about Mark. As a matter of fact, he was on my mind all night. I couldn't wait to see him in school the next day. I fell asleep dreaming about him and being in love. I always wanted to feel loved by a man and thought that Mark might be the one.

Fast forward, two years later, I was shocked to learn that I was pregnant. I never dreamed that I would be a teen mom. I couldn't tell my parents or my best friend, Kim. I sure didn't want to tell Mark about the pregnancy. I pondered, "What am I going to do?" I loved Mark. When his heart beat, my heart beat. He was my everything. Mark asked if we could have sex, and at first I was scared, but I eventually gave in. We started out kissing and then we started touching. I was so in love. If Mark told me to jump off the cliff, I would have done it.

The first time we had sex, it hurt, and blood was all over the sheets. We had sex at least four times a week. He made me feel loved and special. Sometimes he'd buy me a nice gift because he worked at the burger joint. I was getting bigger, and soon my secret would be out. I wore two girdles to hold my stomach in so no one could see my big stomach. Finally, I couldn't hide it any longer; I had to tell my parents. Mom was hurt when I told her because she had high hopes for me. She cried all weekend. Dad really didn't say too much, but I could tell he was hurt too. I was mad about being pregnant but also happy.

Soon, I gave birth to a baby boy. We named him Solomon Lee. He was the most beautiful baby ever. Mark was a proud father. He told me that he was joining the military when he graduated, and after I finished high school, we would get married. I was not ready to be a mother, but I did the best I knew how. Mom helped out a lot; she really took over, and I really didn't mind.

Mark and I eventually returned to church. Unfortunately, we had to stand in front of the whole church and ask for forgiveness because we had a baby and were not married. The church forgave us. Later, I thought to myself, "We didn't have to ask the church nothing as long as we asked God for forgiveness."

7

The Happiest Day

Mark and I were in love with a beautiful son. Solomon smiled just like his daddy, and that melted my heart. Apart from the joy, deep down inside, I was not ready to be a teen mom. Happily, I had a lot of support. My mom gladly cared for Solomon, and sometimes Mark's parents watched the baby. Both sides of the family spoiled him. My friend Kim came around to help me. Her mom bought nice gifts for the baby. Mark got a job working at a burger joint. Sometimes when he got off from work late he came to see me.

My son wore nothing but name brand clothes. Mark and I stayed together trying to make each other happy. It was the perfect family. Nevertheless, I still felt like something was missing in my life, but I could not put my finger on it. I was still having sex, and Mom finally put me on birth control pills. I was OK with her decision because I didn't want any more children.

My dad got drunk more often than usual. I guess he was disappointed that I was a teen mom, but he never said anything. If he had taken the time to love me, maybe my life would have been different.

It was time for Mark to graduate from high school. I was sad because he was leaving school. I knew that I would miss him walking me to class. On the other hand, I was happy that he was out of high school. One day we took a walk to the park because he told me that he had something to tell me. At first I was scared. I thought he was breaking up with me. Instead, he told me that he was joining the Navy to make a better life for us. All I could do was smile. I gave him a big kiss. We talked about marriage and, even though we were young, I didn't care; I wanted to be with him.

The Graduation ceremony was nice. I was sad because my love was leaving, and I was stuck behind in this hell of a world. He told me that he would be back to get us, and that made my heart smile. The day came when Mark was off to defend his country. It was a sad day. We said our goodbyes, and then I gave him a kiss. As he was leaving to get on the bus, I called out his name and then ran to him. I whispered in his ear, "I love you, and I will be here waiting on you." I felt that God had sent me a soul mate. Shortly, the letters started coming from Mark. I wrote my baby at least three times a week, and he wrote me back. I got two letters a week from Mark.

Dear My Love,

I'm missing you so much. How are you doing? Our son is fine, he's growing like crazy. I can't wait to see you, touch you, kiss you, and you know the rest. I think of you all the time. You are the apple of my eye. Please be safe.

Love always

I felt that my world was upside down without Mark. I thought about him constantly. One day I got a letter from him that said, "Let's get married and make it official." I felt like the luckiest girl on earth. I knew I was too young to get married, but this was my last year in high school. All I wanted to do was graduate, so that I could leave Alabama and get out of my parents' house.

While some of my friends were making plans to go off to college, my focus was on Mark. Kim was planning on going to Spelman College in Georgia, and her boyfriend was going to Morris Brown. I felt like Kim was acting funny towards me. We used to talk every day, but now we talked only once a week. It didn't really bother me because I was on cloud nine thinking of Mark.

My dad did not attend my graduation. I was hurt because all my friends' fathers were there. Mom came; I was certain she would be there even though she was disappointed that I was a teen mom. Mom loved helping out with the baby, and one time I heard her say that Solomon was her son. I thought to myself, "What is this lady talking about? Has she been hitting the gin bottle?"

Kim's whole family attended the graduation. I felt a little jealous, but I quickly got over it. My high school had the most beautiful ceremony. After graduation, Mom took us out to eat. It was a nice day, but deep down inside I was sad because Mark was not here. After graduation, Kim invited me to her graduation party. Her family threw a really big party at her house. Mom decided to come with me to the party. Mark's mom watched the baby. Kim's party had all kinds of delicious foods. The decorations were beautiful and on point. She even had a DJ. Lots of kids came over to the party. We danced and we ate.

I spent the night at Kim's house. During our girl talk time, I told her that I was getting married. She had a weird look on her face. She told me that I was making a big mistake and that I should focus on my education. I was trying not to hear a word she was saying. After telling Kim that I was getting married, I started telling a lot more people. Some people were happy and some were against it. Mark's mom and aunt urged me to wait until I got a little older. I was so in love with Mark that I couldn't hear a word people were trying to tell me. Sadly, I couldn't hear what God was trying to tell me either.

Slowly, letters stopped coming on a regular basis from Mark. I was only getting a letter once a week and felt that something was wrong. I started having crazy dreams about a man and a lady having a baby. The weird thing about the dream was that I was standing beside the lady, having a baby too. The dream scared me so bad I woke up crying.

8

The Sign Was There

I woke up crying with my mind racing with all kinds of thoughts about Mark. My love can't be cheating. He told me that he loved me and that me and the baby were moving with him to Hawaii. In the midst of this, I decided to stop and pray. Afterwards, I felt a little better, but deep down inside I had a weird feeling. The phone rang and Mom answered the phone. I heard her say, "Hello, Mark, how are things going? Is the military life treating you good? That's good. Hold on. Natasha, telephone, it's your beau!" I ran to the phone so fast you would have thought I was in the Olympics. "Hi, Baby, how's it going? I've been missing you," I said. Hearing Mark's voice made me feel so good. He told me that he missed me and wanted me and the baby to come for a weekend visit in Texas. Mark was stationed in Austin, Texas. He said that he would send some money so that I could buy a bus ticket. I asked, "When are we leaving?" He said, "The next weekend I am off, I want to see you and the baby." We talked for about an hour, but I could have talked to my love all day. Before we said goodbye, he said, "I will send you the money tomorrow through Western Union." "OK, Love," I replied. Mark told me that he loved me, and I told him that I loved him too, and we ended the call. As I hung up the phone, I had an unsettling feeling. All I could say was, "What is it, God?" God didn't answer me.

I told Mom about my conversation with Mark; she was happy for me. She asked, "Have you set a wedding date?" "Not yet," I replied. I told her that I am tossing around the idea of doing a courthouse wedding and then having a big reception." Mom said, "That sounds good."

I called Kim to tell her about my trip to Texas. She didn't sound happy; I brushed it off. I was too happy to care how she felt. As I continued talking about Mark, Kim said, "You are moving too fast." I'm not sure why she said that. She had a boyfriend; therefore, I could not understand why she couldn't be happy for me. Kim asked if I wanted to go out to eat and do a little shopping. I was making my own money by working at Wendy's, so I was all in for an evening on the town. In addition to my paycheck, Mark sent me around $250 a month. Kim and I walked around the mall for a while before deciding to dine at Red Lobster. I brought my son, Solomon, with me to the mall. Wherever I went, my son went too. Kim loved to be around Solomon. At dinner, we excitedly talked about our plans to leave Alabama and start a new life. Kim was moving to Atlanta to start college in three months. I was moving to Texas next summer after the wedding to pursue a nursing career. I liked helping people and had a passion to care for the elderly.

The weekend for me and Solomon to travel to Texas was finally here. Mom took us to the bus station. I was elated; it was my first time going out of town by myself. We rode the Greyhound bus. It stopped in every small town- nerve wracking! My six hour trip turned into a nine hour trip. After that long ride, I was determined never to ride Greyhound again. As soon as we arrived to our destination, I started looking immediately for Mark. We arrived thirty minutes early, but I knew he would be there waiting for us. I could hardly wait to see my man. After forty-five minutes of waiting, there stood the love of my life. I was smiling so hard you would have thought that I was the Kool-Aid kid.

When I saw him, I forgot all about the forty-five minutes he kept us waiting. One of his Navy buddies gave him a ride to pick us up. We drove to the hotel. My love did have a little taste; we stayed in the "Hilton Garden." The rooms were so nice. That was the second time I stayed in a hotel. I wanted to kiss my man all night, but I did bring the baby with me. Mark took us to dinner, then to the mall.

I was in Heaven, but I couldn't get over an uneasy feeling that lingered with me all that day. I asked God, "What is it, Lord?" I prayed, "Lord, please let this be a safe and happy trip." After dinner we went back to the room. Mark played around with the baby, and I watched television. It was great to be in Texas with my love. I daydreamed about what our life would be once we were married. Around 8:00 pm, the phone rang. I wasn't expecting a call because I talked to my mother earlier that day. We let the phone ring until it stopped. Thirty minutes later, Mark said, "I am going to step outside to call my boss." I replied, "At this hour?"

I was so stupid in love that I was not thinking clearly. I should have asked, "Why are you going outside to make a phone call? There is a phone in the room." An hour passed and Mark had not returned to the room, I was getting worried. I heard a knock on the door, and when I looked to see who it was, it was the police. The officer asked,

"Do you know a Mark Brown?" I said, "Yes sir." I asked the officer if something was wrong. The officer said, "Mark has been arrested for fighting a female around the corner, and we have him in the police car." I was in shock. The officer allowed me to see him. By this time, I was scared and crying. I asked Mark, "What is going on?" He said, "Some lady I met at a friend's house is stalking me. She came to the hotel to borrow some money, and I told her that my family was here. She got mad and tried to fight me."

I was so naïve, I believed him. I pleaded with the officer to let him go. The officer let Mark go perhaps because I wouldn't stop crying, and I told him that I was from out of town. Mark got out of the car and tried to hold my hand, but I pulled back and went inside the room. He tried to explain again and I listened to him. Solomon was asleep. We kissed and made love like never before. I was on cloud nine. The next morning it was time to go back home. We said our goodbyes.

It was the longest bus ride home. That uneasy feeling was back again, and I asked, "What is it, God?" I called Kim and told her about my trip and the incident that occurred with my love. Kim told me to watch my heart. Weeks passed and I had not heard from Mark. No letter or phone call. I heard a voice tell me that it was over. I heard it but didn't give it any attention. I thought that the voice was Satan trying to make me unhappy. Three months passed, and I was so worried that something had happened to my love. I heard the phone ring, and when I answered, it was my love on the phone. "Hey, Love, what's going on with you?" he asked. I said, "OK, why have there been no phone calls or letters from you?" I could hear it in his voice that it was over. He said, "Natasha, I can't be with you; I'm in love with someone else." I could do nothing but scream to the top of my lungs, "Why, what did I do? Please tell me. You mean everything to me. You are my first love, the only man that I had sex with. I love you, I love you. Let's work it out." Mark said, "No, Natasha, we can't; I'm sorry for hurting you." I asked, "What about our son? What about us, Mark?" He said, "I'm sorry; she needs me. Goodbye, Natasha."

I threw the phone down and fell to the floor in tears. You would have thought that my best friend had died the way I was acting out. It felt like someone ripped my heart out and walked on it. After all that I put in the relationship…this is what I got? I asked God, "Why, God? Why don't you see me?" I wanted to die, I wanted to commit suicide. I ran to the bathroom, grabbed a bottle of pills, and swallowed the whole bottle of pills. I went to my room and got in bed. The next morning, I woke up throwing up all over my bed. I started thinking, "I took the wrong pills; damn Tylenol, God doesn't love me."

43

9

Is There Life After Pain?

Dad called me in his room to pray. He asked me to get on my knees, and as I knelt down, he started to pray. He prayed, "Heavenly Father, please take away my daughter's pain. Take away all of the hurt and give her back Your peace and watch over her. In Jesus' name, Amen. I felt a little better, but all I could do was think about Mark and ask myself, "Where did I go wrong? Did I say something? Did I not write enough? Was my love-making bad? Please, somebody help me."

I was glad that I didn't die that night from the overdose of Tylenol because I might have gone to hell. I've heard people say when you commit suicide, you go to hell, and I knew I didn't want to be in hell. I simply wanted to go to sleep and wake up and my nightmare would be over. I wanted to wake up, but soon I realized I was awake in a real reality moment in my life. I forgot I had a son to raise, and suicide should not have been an option.

I am so thankful to God for my support team. My mom stepped in at the right time in my life. I went into a deep depression, and no one knew it because I hid it from people. I couldn't eat and lost weight very fast. Being around people made me sick. Listening to slow music made me cry. It was slow jams like Aaliyah's "Let Me Know" that tore me up inside. Tears ran down my face like a waterfall as I listened to the song. The words, "Let me know, let me know, let me know. When I feel sometimes, what I feel it's hard to tell you so. You may not be in the mood to learn what you think you know. There are times when I find you want to keep yourself from me." I had to pull my car over and cry. I prayed, "Lord, help me. Do you hear me? Do you care? Can you see my pain?"

I got a call from my best friend, Kim. She said, "Hey, Natasha, I haven't heard from you in weeks. Are you OK?" "No, what do you want? I can't talk right now." I hung up the phone and ran to my room. Mom was at church at this time. I was not attending church. I was not in the mood to hear no lying preacher talk about love, Jesus, and heaven. I felt these words were a lie because my pain would not go away.

I felt so stupid. Living in a small town, all you get is people in other people's business, and they don't know what they're talking about. People were looking at me sideways and whispering. I wanted to tell them where to go and hide their ugly face, but I just let them talk. Kim came over two days later to see me. I heard a knock at the door but was not interested in talking with anyone. When I realized that it was Kim, I asked, "What do you want? Go away I'm not in the mood today." She said, "Girl, open this door and stop being silly." I opened the door, and all I could do was hug and cry for about four minutes. We went to my room. I told her what happened. She wiped my face and told me that I was going to be OK. She said, "That idiot doesn't deserve you. You deserve better. He will pay for how he treated you and your son." I was grateful for her words of comfort, but I said, "Kim, the love I had for him you just don't know." Kim invited me to dinner and I accepted. Afterwards I felt a little better. Getting out of the house for a while took my mind off of Mark.

Christmas was right around the corner. By this time my mom and dad had stopped fighting, but the screaming did not. I could deal with the screaming. I was glad the fighting stopped. I believe the fighting stopped because one night Mom came home and Dad wanted to fight. He was screaming at the top of his lungs. Suddenly, Dad pulled back and knocked Mom to the floor. I ran outside to my aunt's house to get help. I knocked on my auntie's door hard and fast. She yelled, "What is it?" I said, "Mom and Dad are fighting; come quickly." We ran back towards the house. As we approached the house, I heard Dad screaming as if he was in severe pain. Mom had thrown hot fish grease on his chest. After that incident, there was no more fighting.

One day Mom went to the grocery store to buy food for dinner and got the surprise of her life. She saw Mark and his new wife, Wendy. Mom was never one to hold back on words, and she had quite a few choice words for Mark. She asked Mark, "What the hell is going on?" He replied, "Hey, Mrs. Lee, this is my wife, Wendy. We got married last week, and these are my kids." He had four children with him. Mom asked, "Why did you make my daughter think that you were going to marry her? Did you forget about your son, Solomon?" She asked Wendy, "Don't you know about Lily?" She tried to get smart, but Mom told her to shut her mouth before she put her fist in it. "Now, Mrs. Lee, you wrong!" Mom said, "No, you are wrong. God will pay you back, just you see." Mom said they ran out of the store so fast you would have thought that they were running from fire. Mom returned home, looking crazy. She sat me down and said, "Natasha, I just seen your ex, and he was with his new wife." Those words cut deep. Tears filled my eyes and ran down my cheeks. Mom told me to wipe my face and pull myself together. She told me to let God deal with Mark. I told Mom, "You don't know how I feel." She quickly blurted, "Yes, I do. I caught your dad in bed with another woman one night, so don't tell me I don't know pain, little girl. I lived through pain, OK."

I asked Mom, "What did he say when he saw you?" "He stood there, looking stupid like he had seen a ghost," Mom said. "Mark was with his four little crumb snatchers and his wife." I yelled, "Wife?," and Mom replied, "Yes, he is married. His wife looked like a man; I was thinking, did he turn gay? She was black as night and tried to get smart, but I asked her if she wanted to taste my fist. She backed down and closed her face up."

"Natasha, you are too beautiful to waste your energy on Mark." Hearing Mom say those words made me feel good; however, I was still angry. I wanted to go to his mom's house and stick a knife in her and him, and whoever got in my way would get it, too. I called his mom's house. His mom answered the phone, and I asked her to put Mark on the phone. When Mark answered the phone, I said, "You think you are smart. How could you move in with your mom? I'm on my way to see you." I slammed the phone in his ear. I got in my car and went to see him. By the time I got there, he was gone. It had to be God who intervened because what I was going to do, I'm sure I would have landed to jail.

You don't know pain unless you have experienced it. One day while listening to the radio, I heard a Betty Wright song, "After the Pain." Well, I couldn't resist the urge to tell you the end of my story. For those who wanted to know was there life after the pain: "After the pain, you come love me and I welcome you. You're a glad sight to see." That song stayed with me.

10

I Started Over

I started to live a life where I really didn't care about anyone or anything. I had seen my father mistreat my mother. I had no role model to tell or show me what to look for in a man. All I saw was abuse, and to me that was love. I started to party every weekend, drink like a fish, and disrespect my body. I allowed men to abuse me mentally. Kim and I would go to the club and party all night. She really wasn't a drinker like me, and that was cool because I needed a designated driver. Sometimes I didn't leave the club until the DJ packed up. I was trying to find something to take away my heartache.

One Friday night I was in the club, sitting at the bar, grooving to the beat, and sipping on some gin and juice, my favorite drink, when a tall man came up and started to talk with me. He smelled so good and he had the prettiest smile. He asked my name and instead of telling him, I got smart with the brother. He told me that he saw me alone and deep in thought, so he decided to come over and ask if I would like another drink. I started to loosen up. I asked, "What's your name?" He said, "Todd, nice to meet you." I said, "My name is Natasha." He started to talk but I told him, "Don't start all that talking. I'm drinking gin with grapefruit juice." He told the bartender to get two more of what I'm drinking. I must say the brother was nice. He asked me would I like to dance, and I said sure. A slow song by "Atlantis Starr" was playing. I needed to hear that song because that was how I was feeling that night. I was all alone and needed someone to lift my spirit. When we danced, he held me tight. For one night, I forgot about my heartache and Mark.

Todd lifted my spirit that night. We danced until the club closed. As we were leaving the club, he asked, "Do you want some breakfast?" I asked if he was trying to get some booty. He said, "No, I just want to eat with you. What's open in this town at 4:00 am?" I said, "You must not be from around here because the only thing open is Waffle House." "I moved here three months ago," he replied.

I did not like Waffle House, but I could eat some toast and get a coffee. He walked me to my car and asked if I was OK to drive. I was fine to drive. We made it to the Waffle House, and he was a perfect gentleman. We talked for at least three hours. I learned that he relocated here with his job and was ex-military. I asked, "Where do you live?" He said, "About four miles from here." I gave him my number. I went home thinking about my night. At home, Mom was up making coffee. For some reason, she got up with the chickens. "Where have you been?" Mom blurted out. I didn't feel like talking, but I couldn't disrespect my mom. I said, "Mom, I met this nice man and we went to breakfast. It was just what I needed. I forgot all about Mark for one night." Mom had a strange look on her face and then said, "Be careful."

I went to my room thinking about this man and wondering when he was going to call. I couldn't wait until sunrise to call Kim and tell her about my night. I heard the doorbell ring. My dad answered the door. It was a flower delivery man with two dozen roses. He said, "Is Lily here? I have a delivery for her." I ran downstairs yelling, "What is it, Dad? "A gift for you," he replied. I signed for the roses. It had a card enclosed that read, "Thanks for last night. Kiss, Todd." The smile on my face was priceless. As I was caught up in the moment, the phone rang, and it was Todd. He said, "Hi, pretty lady, did you get my gift?" "Yes," I replied. "How did you know where I live?" He said, "I followed you home because I wanted to make sure that you got home safe. I'm calling to see if you are free tonight. I forgot to tell you that I have a three-year-old son." "That's cool," I thought. "I'll meet him one day." He asked, "Where is Daddy Navy?" I said, "We are not together anymore- long story."

He called to invite me to dinner. He found a restaurant on the river and thought it would be a perfect place for dinner. Before hanging up, he said, "Natasha, I'm not going to do anything to you. I just see something that I like. I'm not dating anyone, how about you?" I answered, "No, I haven't been on a date since my ex left me." As I hung up the phone, I saw Mom around the corner being nosy, but it was cool. She asked me why I was smiling so hard. I told her that I had a date with Todd, the nice man I met at the club. Mom asked, "Did you forget that you have a son?" "No," I replied. "I love this baby with all of my heart, but can you watch him for me tonight, right?" Mom said, "I guess." I thanked Mom and ran to my room to pick out my date outfit.

As I was looking through my closet, I kept saying to myself, "Thank God for my job; I can buy my own clothes." It was summer time, but I checked the television to see the temperature; it was going to be 84 degrees. I decided to wear a nice yellow halter top dress complimented by some cute red flats. To kill time waiting for Todd, I played with my son, gave him a bath, and then put him to bed. I almost lost track of time. At 6:30 pm, I ran to take a shower and put on my lotion and smell goods. You couldn't tell me that I wasn't looking hot. I grabbed my purse; by this time it was 7:15 pm. I heard someone at the door. I heard Mom say, "May I help you?" I yelled, "Mom, this is Todd." I introduced Todd to my mother, and he said, "I see where you get your beauty." He drove a nice, black, sports car, and when he opened my car door, there was a yellow rose on the seat. I was in heaven. We pulled up to the restaurant, and it was a beautiful place. Excited, I said, "I always wanted to come here." "Well, your wish has come true," he replied.

The waitress put us at a table with a lake view. After we placed our drink order, Todd said, "Tell me more about you." I asked, "What do you want to know?" "What do you like? What makes you smile?" We talked for hours. Deep down inside, I couldn't believe that I had met a nice man. "Did God send him to me?" I never felt that I was worthy to date a man so kind. After dinner, we walked up and down the lake. Funny how time flies when you're having fun. I did tell him how Mark broke my heart. He told me that he was not here to hurt me and then leaned over and gave me a kiss.

It had been so long since a man kissed me. We kissed for three minutes. It was soon time to go home. It was late, and I had to go to work the next day. Todd walked me to the door and kissed me good night. He told me that he will call me tomorrow, and he thinks that a movie will be a nice date. I told him that I will let him know. As I walked in the house, I said, "God, if this is not You, please give me a sign." I went to bed with a smile on my face and feeling great. If I was dreaming, I did not want anyone to wake me up; let me stay asleep, in Jesus' name.

11

He Loves Me

I was so happy that a man like Todd wanted to date me. He had his own house, nice car, and he was handsome. He told me that he moved here with his job, but later he told me that his family owns an Accounting firm, and he helps his family. Todd took my mind off Mark; the pain was slowly leaving. Deep down, I felt unworthy to date a man like Todd. My self-esteem was low, and I was very insecure. In front of people, I smiled, trying to make people love me.

Kim was leaving for college, and I really didn't want her to leave. We became friends in elementary school. We did everything together. Kim felt a little jealous because I was spending time with Todd a lot. I forgot all about Kim and focused my time on Todd. I also forgot that I had a son. I wanted to feel loved. The pain from childhood coupled with a man walking out on me left me cold and bitter. I really couldn't give Todd one hundred percent of me because I really didn't know how. He showed me that he cared about me. Whatever I wanted, I got.

One night Todd invited me over to his home. He stayed in a gated community. He surprised me with dinner and a nice diamond bracelet. I was speechless! A man had not made me feel this good in a long time. He poured me a glass of wine. As we sat down for dinner I asked, "Baby, did you cook this for me?" "Yes, Mama," he replied. He had cooked a delicious meal of grilled salmon, asparagus, salad, and fruit with whipped topping for dessert. The meal was fantastic. When we got together, we talked all night. The inside of his home was so nice. You would think that a woman stayed with him. After dinner, we watched a movie. He leaned over and started to kiss me. Boy, he was a great kisser. I asked him where this relationship was going and what he wanted from me. He said, "I want to be with you- only you. I knew you were the one the night I saw you at the club. Something about your smile just lit up the whole room. You have the most beautiful spirit."

I told him that my diamond bracelet was nice. I asked, "Why did you buy me this bracelet?" He replied, "A lady deserves the finer things in life, and I have more gifts for you to come. We went into the bedroom and the lovemaking was magical. A man hadn't touched me in a year. Todd made me feel so good. I ended up spending the night. His bed was so soft I could have slept there all day. At 7:00 am, I kissed him goodbye and he walked me to my car. He asked me to call him later.

Driving home, I felt so bad, sick to my stomach. I thought, "What have I done? I just met this man three months ago." I kept telling myself that this man doesn't want me because I was not worthy to have a man like him. God, what's wrong with me?

Kim's family gave her a going-away party, and I went just to see my best friend off to college. Kim's family always gave nice parties. As I was going to the restroom, a fine man was standing by the door. He asked, "What's your name?" I smiled and told him. This man was drop dead gorgeous. We talked for about 30 minutes, and before I knew it, we were in the upstairs bathroom going at it. He pulled my skirt up and placed his manhood inside of me. I really enjoyed the crazy sex, but afterwards I felt nasty. "What the hell did you just do?" I asked myself. I wasn't thinking about Todd's feelings or mine. All I knew was the man I banged in the bathroom was Kim's uncle, and he was married. To make matters worse, she was downstairs enjoying the party. No one missed us, but it was too close for comfort. I thought about how trifling I was.

Todd kept blowing up my phone. Eventually, I had to take his call. When I answered, he said, "Hey, Baby, how are you?" "I'm good," I replied. He told me that he had been calling me most of the day, and I told him that my phone needed charging. He asked, "What is the noise in the background?" I told him that I was at a friend's going-away party. He got a little quiet and said, "You should have invited me." I replied, "I thought that you had to work today." I told him that I was not going to be staying long; I had to work in the morning. He asked me to stop by on my way home, but I told him that I was too sleepy to drive. The real reason I did not want to stop by was because of my bathroom escapade with a stranger. I felt nasty.

My drinking started to get out of hand. I stopped going to work. All I wanted to do was drink, party, and have sex. Why did I choose this life? I chose it because no one taught me about self-love, and I never saw love in my life. Morning had come, and I was still in bed, sick to my stomach. I couldn't keep anything down. My period was late, but I just couldn't be pregnant. I was not in a state of mind to have a baby. There was no room in my life for a baby. Furthermore, I had slept with three other men besides Todd; I didn't know who the father was.

I made a doctor's appointment that day to see the doctor. As I was lying across the bed, there was a knock at the door. I went to the door and asked, "Who is it?" "It's me, Baby, Todd." I opened the door and told him that I was not in the mood for him today. He was looking good and had a huge smile. He asked, "What's up?" I said, "I'm feeling sick to my stomach. I'm going to the doctor at 1:00 pm to let them check me out." He asked, "When did you have your last period?" "Two months ago," I said. He replied, "Well, Baby, you might be having our baby." I fired back, "I don't want kids now. It is bad timing, and one child is enough to take care of without a husband." He said, "Who said you have to do it by yourself? I'm here, and I love you with all my heart." I didn't want to continue the conversation, so I told him that I needed to get ready for my appointment.

He hugged me and asked if he could drive me to the doctor and grab lunch afterwards. I consented, and he drove me to my appointment. I filled out so many papers. It took me forty-five minutes to check in and complete my paperwork before they called me back to see the doctor. When I was called back, the nurse asked me to put some urine in a cup. Shortly thereafter, the doctor came in and told me that I was three months pregnant. I could have hit the floor. I had to pull myself together because no one could know this. I came back to the reception area where Todd was waiting, with a big smile on my face. I gave him a kiss and said, "There is no baby; it's a stomach virus."

We decided to find a seafood place for lunch. I was not thinking about food. My mind was racing to locate an abortion clinic by Monday. In the meantime, Tom, the married guy was blowing up my phone. I was feeling bad because I had the best sex with him even though he had a wife and two kids. I really didn't care about his family. I loved the way he made me feel in bed. He talked so nasty and freaky - just what I liked. Sometimes Tom and I went to some of his guy friends' house parties so we could have wild sex in the bathroom. He complained about his wife, but I told him that I didn't care what she does; please spare me the drama.

I had the abortion on Monday, but I felt bad. It was very painful and I bled badly. I had to pay $1,500 because I was three months pregnant. I drove myself to the clinic so no one knew what I was doing.

I didn't want to give people any time to judge me. I prayed, "Lord, I just ask that You please forgive me for what I did today and for all of the lies. Please help me, God. In Jesus' name, Amen." After my prayer, I drank a whole bottle of rum and went to sleep.

12

Why Me, Lord?

The next morning, a loud knock at the door woke me up. The rapid sound of the knocking on the door made me think that it might be the police. "Who is it?" I yelled at the top of my lungs. A voice yelled back, "It's Todd, Honey." I thought to myself, "Lord, what does he want?" What I wanted to do is go back to bed and sleep. When I opened the door he said, "Hey, Baby, I have been calling you all morning, but you did not answer." I said, "My phone must be turned off. What time of day is it?" Todd said, "It's 2:00 pm. How are you feeling?" I said, "Oh, my, I slept ten hours. I've got a little stomach pain; it's that time of the month. I'll be OK; I will take some Ibuprofen."

I couldn't tell Todd that I had an abortion yesterday. Lord, please help me. Todd said, "I came by to check on you and to see if you needed anything. Do you want to grab some lunch or go for a ride? It's a nice day and I'm off work." I couldn't tell him that I didn't want to go to lunch because I have put him off for about two weeks straight. I have been working and trying to date three men at a time. Juggling three men was taking its toll on my body and mind.

I don't know why I was sleeping with all these men. Todd was the perfect gentleman. I had everything a woman needed in a man. Nevertheless, I was just trying to find something that I had been missing my whole life. When I went to take a shower, blood was everywhere. I cleaned myself up, put on some nice-smelling perfume, and I was good to go out. As we were leaving the house, Todd leaned over and kissed me. I wanted to up-chuck, but I played it off.

Todd was taking me to a very nice restaurant downtown where we could sit outside and eat. On the ride to the restaurant, all I could think about was going home and getting back into bed. When we arrived at the restaurant, I went to the restroom. I left my phone on the table. While I was away, I received a text that read, "Are you coming over?" As I was returning to the table, I saw Todd reading my text messages. He was making a frown on his face, and he looked as if he had seen a ghost. When I sat down he asked, "What's going on, Natasha? Do you care to explain?" "What are you talking about?" I asked. Todd said, "A man named Joe just texted you, asking if you are coming over. Why did he ask you that?" I told him to give me my phone, please.

I was busted and did not know how to lie my way out. Joe was a guy that I met at the gas station. I slept with him only three times. He told me that he had a wife and two kids. I really didn't care about his wife or kids. He said that he stays married because of the kids. I have found that all married men tell that stupid lie. His marriage was not an issue for me. I was with him for the crazy sex. He didn't spend any money on me because he said that he had to take care of his kids. What a fool I was!

I told Todd that Joe was some guy at work that was trying to date me. I told him that I have a special someone, but he still calls me. We finished our lunch, and he took me home. However, things didn't feel the same after the text. As I was getting out of Todd's car at home, Larry was calling. He wanted to know if we could hang out. Larry was on the wild side. He sold drugs but never had any money. On our first date, we went to a fish bar. I ordered a $10.00 fish sandwich; he got a beer, and he didn't want to pay the tab. I felt so nasty sleeping with a man for a fish sandwich-what a waste.

I found out that Marcus was spying on me at night. Todd had just left, and this rat-face named Clarence Williams pulled up. He said, "I just seen your man leave. If I find him here with you again, I will use my 357 black." Boy, was I scared! This ninja is crazy. I had to leave him alone. I don't need this type of trouble.

The next morning, I felt this painful feeling in my spirit like something was going to happen to me. I prayed about it. I only prayed when I thought something bad was going to happen. I started hanging out with this group of girls, so-called friends. We bar hopped five times a week. I forgot I had a son or a job.

Todd broke up with me. He couldn't take my trifling butt anymore. He caught me with Joe at my apartment, and I really couldn't lie my way out of this one. After the breakup with Todd, I started back drinking and clubbing from Sunday to Sunday. I was turning it up in strip clubs, restaurants, even a backyard cook-out. I started hanging with these two girls from my job. Both were nurses, and they had nice homes and nice cars. They were very pretty girls. I wanted to be like them. To me, they had it going on.

I partied so much that I lost my job and forgot that I had a son. My life was a rollercoaster ride. We drank Remy Martin like it was water. One of my friends smoked a little pot but nothing major. I didn't get into drugs because I couldn't breathe well.

One morning, on my way home from the nightclub, I found a yellow letter on my front door. It read "eviction" in big black letters. I had no job and no money because all the men that I was sleeping with didn't give a care about me. They just wanted to get off and feel good. I was just a toilet they used to empty their waste. They bought me a drink, maybe food, but deep down I was the biggest fool out there. While I was partying, I lost all of my nice stuff. My two friends Pam and Trina were going home and to work, and they knew how to balance their life, but poor me, I was just going where the wind blew. I wanted that party life…no joke!

Joe came by my apartment to have sex and drink. I couldn't say no because I needed his help. I asked him to loan me $800 to pay my rent. He told me that he had it. Joe and I drank and then had sex. I felt so nasty this time. Abruptly, there was a loud knock on the door. When I looked out, I saw that it was the Sheriff Department coming to evict me. I ran back to the room and asked Joe, "Do you have the $800 I asked for?" He looked at me and said, "No, I forgot to tell you last night."

The Sheriff evicted me. That dog got out of my bed, put his clothes on, and left. I called my mom and told her what was going on. She came over to help. By the time she arrived, three Mexicans were throwing my stuff out like it was trash. I went to the leasing office to see if I could pay my rent and still keep my place. There was an angel there that day. The leasing office worked with me, and by the time I got back to my place, the television was gone. My microwave, end table, and my shoes were gone. I said, "God, can You hear my cry today?" One of the maintenance men helped me put my stuff back in my apartment.

That day I felt lower then low. Mom was lecturing me, and I didn't want to hear what she was saying. Sternly she said, "My child, you need to pull yourself together, and whatever you doing must stop. God is calling your name, but you just can't hear Him - too busy in these streets thinking you doing something, but all you're doing is making a mess of the life God gave you. Where are those so-called friends? Please don't let me start on these men you mess with. God blessed you with a good man, but you didn't have a clue what to do with him; now he's long gone." "You talk with him yesterday?" "Natasha, you hurt that man bad, and he will never come back to you." Tears just rolled down my face. Mom asked, "Do you remember you gave birth to a baby son named Solomon?" No words could come out my mouth. My mom got up and headed to the door. She looked at me and said, "I want my money back."

13
I Lied

The next morning my phone rang, and it was Joe on the other end. I yelled, "What do you want with me, Joe? I asked your lying self for help, and you just left me hanging. Please don't call my phone anymore." Joe yelled, "Wait, wait, Tasha. I was scared because I didn't want my wife to know that I was at another woman's house." I screamed back, "How in the hell was your wife going to find out? The sheriff that came to the door was her cousin, so don't give me that bull."

He kept talking, and for some reason I started to believe him. I finally gave in and told him that I would meet him, but he was going to give me some gas money. I met Joe at a hole in the wall dive. We had drinks and laughed. All of a sudden, I noticed a man across the room was looking at me as if I was a piece of meat on a stick. I played it off and told Joe that I needed to use the restroom and that I would be right back. On my way to the bathroom, the man followed me into the ladies room. The bathroom only had one stall. I asked, "How can I help you?" He said, "I see you over there with that lame of a man." "What's it to you?" I asked. He said, "I was wondering if you would like to make some money." "How would I do that? What is your name?" He replied, "My name is Will." He gave me his number and told me to call him later to get the details. When I returned to Joe, he wanted to know what took me so long to get back. I gave him a mean look that made him shut up. Joe was a little slow, but I didn't care because his sex was good, and that kept me with him.

By the time I got home, my head was hurting from stressing out about how I was going to get next month's rent. Since I needed some money, I decided to call Will. When he answered the phone, I said, "Hi, Will, this is Natasha, the woman you met in the bathroom." He said, "Hey, pretty lady. I have some friends who are having a party. You should come over and dance." I asked, "What did you say?" He said, "Come over and dance. You looked like a dancer, and they need a little of your time." My mind was racing in all directions. I needed money for rent, food, and a whole host of other stuff. I asked, "Where is this party and how much are they paying?"

Will gave me the address, and the next week I was over there. When I walked up in the place, it seemed as if I was walking into the movie,

Player's Club. I immediately saw about five guys drinking and playing cards. I didn't know any of them. I walked towards the bedroom, and as I was entering, a lady came out of the bathroom and asked, "What's your name?" I asked her the same question, "What is your name?" She answered, "Nicole". She said, "Hey, are you here to make some money?" "I guess," I replied. She said, "Men come over to play cards and have sex with random women. Girl, get all you can get." I told her that Will asked me to come and dance. She said, "Girl, Will is full of mess. These guys want sex." Suddenly, a tall guy came in the room with his pants down and said, "Hey Baby, are you ready?" I looked at him and said, "Hell, no, ready for what?" He pulled out a stack of money, and all I saw was rent money and food and I was all in. I didn't know the man's name. Even though he was on top of me, I really couldn't feel anything because he had a small penis. I gave my body to four men that night. I felt nasty and disgusting.

I made about $500, and it still was not enough to pay my rent. Somewhere in my brain, I tricked myself into thinking that I could start a life of sleeping with men for money. The next month, I had to move out of my apartment. I asked a friend if I could move in with her for a while and she said yes. I put my belongings in storage. Mom didn't like my roommate decision, but my pride wouldn't let me move back home. Honestly, I was so far gone. Whoring was my thing because I felt loved and I was getting money, but in reality, I was making a fool of myself. I was living reckless. If they gave awards for strippers faking orgasms, I could win an Oscar.

One night I was hungry, so I pulled my car up to Red Lobster. I sat in my car watching people walk in and out of the restaurant. Eventually, I got out of my car and went inside. I walked up to the bar and ordered a glass of wine and a crab dinner. I was praying and eating at the same time. I said, "God, I don't know how I'm going to pay for this meal. Please send me some help." Shortly, a tall, chocolate guy walked by me and sat down. He spoke and asked, "What is your name?" I said, "Natasha." He asked if I was eating alone and I said yes. For some reason, a crazy feeling came over me. We talked for at least two hours. The bill came, and he told the waiter that he was going to pay my tab. I could have kissed him because I only had two dollars to my name. He paid the tab and told me to have a blessed night. He walked out the door just like that. As I drove home, I thought about what just happened to me. I began to pray, "God, I really need Your help. I'm about to go crazy. Please give me a sense of direction. Please, Jesus. I lied to my family. I lied to my friends about my lifestyle. What a mess I am making out of my life."

14
The Turnaround

My cell phone rang, and when I answered, a familiar voice said, "Hello, Natasha." It was Kim, my best friend from childhood, whom I loved so much. I realized that my lifestyle made me forget about her. Kim said, "Hey, Natasha, how you doing?" I told her that everything was good. I played it off like I had it going on. I couldn't tell her that I was sleeping in my car at times and whoring around for money just to eat. Kim asked, "Why are you ignoring my phone calls?" She went on to say, "I have been praying for you on a daily basis. I am engaged to Joe, and I want you to be my maid of honor. You don't need to buy anything. My father is paying for everyone's dress and shoes." I hesitated for a minute; then I said, "I would love to be in your wedding." Kim told me that the wedding was next Saturday at 5:00 pm and that she would like for me to come on Thursday. If I arrived on Thursday, we would have a chance to hang out and catch up on old times and meet some of her new friends.

We talked for hours, and during the entire conversation, tears filled my eyes. We hung up, and I thought to myself, "How am I going to get the money to travel to Atlanta?" I began to lay out my options. One option was to sleep with a man and get the money, but the other side of me was saying I can't open my legs no more. I am so tired of that lifestyle. I could not understand how I stooped so low to sell my body to the devil. I felt so nasty. I asked God, "What am I going to do?" I looked in my glove compartment and saw my car title, and a bell went off in my head: I can pawn my title. If I pawned my title, I did not have to sleep with random men. I decided to pawn my car title. They gave me $500 for it. The interest I had to pay back was high. These pawn companies are a rip-off. I cashed the check, and the next week I was off to Atlanta. I didn't have to worry about a place to stay because I was staying with Kim.

For some reason, a strange feeling came over me that I couldn't shake. I asked, "God, are You trying to tell me something?" I did not get an answer so I played it off. Kim's friends were very nice to me. She introduced me as her childhood sister and best friend for life. At one point, I looked up and saw Kim's uncle who I had sex with in the bathroom years ago. I wanted to throw up. He kept staring at me, but I gave him a dirty look that said get lost.

The next morning, Kim's mom made a big breakfast before the wedding. I was feeling a little jealous and wishing that my life was like this and full of joy. Kim had a lot of nice things, and no, I didn't steal anything; I just couldn't do it. The wedding was beautiful. Kim's dad got us rooms at a very nice four star hotel in downtown Atlanta. The next morning around 6:00 am, someone was knocking on my door. I thought to myself that it could not be Housekeeping because checkout was not until 11:00 am. I went to the door and asked, "Who is it?," but there was no answer. I opened the door, and it was Kim's uncle. Before I knew it, I went off on him. I yelled, "What do you want this time of the morning?" He responded, "You." I told him to get his old liniment-smelling behind from my door or I was going to tell his wife on him, and I slammed the door in his face.

At that moment, I said, "No more of this reckless living." I got back in bed and went to sleep. For some reason, I had a scary dream that demons were around my bed, and one part of me was going to hell, and the other part was going to heaven. I woke up with tears in my eyes. I cried, "No more, God; please save me." I fell on my knees and started to cry out to God and pray. I must have been on my knees for hours. Housekeeping entered my room to clean. When I looked up, an elderly black lady was standing by me. She had a beautiful glow on her face. She said, "Baby, it's going to be OK- God's got you. God's going to use you for His glory," and then she walked out of the room." I packed my bags and said my goodbyes to Kim, Joe, and her family. Kim kissed me and said, "Don't stay away anymore."

My ride back home was different. I still had a strange feeling. That day I heard God say, "Go back home." I was done sleeping with different men, drinking, and partying because if I kept it up my soul was hell-bound. I pulled up to my family's house. My mom was sitting on the porch, singing to herself. I ran to my mom, crying like a baby. Mom and I had a tight bond that no one could break, but when you let Satan in, you are doomed. My mom said, "I knew you were on your way back home. I prayed every night and called on God to save my daughter and keep her covered with the blood of Jesus." I said, "Mom, I am so sorry for all the heartache that I have caused you. Please forgive me, please." Mom looked at me and said, "God is going to use you in a special way."

I moved back home, started going to church, and praying more. One day in my room, I turned on the radio and heard Shirley Caesar singing "Jesus, I love calling Your name." That morning, I felt free. A weight was lifted off me. While I was in my mess, Jesus was with me, and, now, I will live and die for Him.

P.O. Box 453

Powder Springs, Georgia 30127

770.727.6517

info@entegritypublishing.com

www.entegritypublishing.com